Renew by phone or online
0845 0020 777
www.bristol.gov.uk/libraries
Bristol Libraries

PLEASE RETURN BOOK BY LAST DATE STAMPED

NOV 08   24. JUL 10.
                    13. JUN 11.
           26. JUL 10.
20. DEC 08.
                           06. AUG 11
23. FEB 09.   14. AUG 10.

24. MAR 09.   16. SEP 10.   25. AUG 11
              07 OCT 10
02. APR 09.
              26. OCT 10   12. SEP 11

10. AUG 09.   0 3 NOV 2010

03. SEP 09. 22. NOV 10.

18. MAR 10.   2 DEC 2010

27 APR 10   FEB 11.

22 JUN 10.
         18. MAR. 11

BRISTOL CITY LIBRARIES
WITHDRAWN AND OFFERED FOR SALE

BR100   21055 Print Servicess

Bristol Libraries

1800059455

D0177847

For Imogen & Phoebe, with love
R.H.

For Smriti, who asked me to do the book
B.C.

BRISTOL CITY LIBRARIES	
AN1800059455	
PE	17-Oct-2008
JF	£10.99

First published in Great Britain in 2008 by Bloomsbury Publishing Plc
36 Soho Square, London, W1D 3QY

Text copyright © by Richard Hamilton 2008
Illustrations copyright © by Babette Cole 2008
The moral rights of the author and illustrator have been asserted

All rights reserved
No part of this publication may be reproduced or
transmitted by any means, electronic, mechanical, photocopying
or otherwise, without the prior permission of the publisher

Designed by Ian Butterworth

A CIP catalogue record of this book is available from the British Library

ISBN 978 0 7475 5249 9

Printed in China

1 3 5 7 9 10 8 6 4 2

All papers used by Bloomsbury Publishing Plc are natural, recyclable products
made from wood grown in well-managed forests. The manufacturing processes
conform to the environmental regulations of the country of origin

www.bloomsbury.com

If I Were You

Richard Hamilton

Illustrated by

Babette Cole

BLOOMSBURY
CHILDREN'S
BOOKS

Dad tucked Daisy up in bed.
   He said, "If I were you, I'd snuggle down and go to sleep."
   "But you're not me," said Daisy.
   "I know . . . but if I were," Dad yawned.

And that set Daisy thinking . . .

"If you were me and I were you," Daisy said,
"I'd read you a story about three bears . . .

then I'd say 'goodnight'
and go downstairs!"

"If you were me and I were you," said Dad,
"I'd go to sleep with Kangaroo,

"If you were me and I were you," said Daisy, "I'd dress you in a **pink tutu!**

I'd give you breakfast ... **porridge**, every day ...

Dad sat up and stroked his chin.

"If you were me – now let me see –
while you washed up, I'd watch TV!

Then I could play with Millie the mouse,
while you made beds and tidied the house!"

Daisy wasn't sure about that!

She said, "Then we'd go out for some fresh air!
And I'd push you in my old pushchair."

"What?" said Dad.
"Past the neighbours? Dressed in pink?
Can you imagine what they'd think?"

"If I were you and you were me," said Daisy,
"I'd take you to the zoo to see
the baby elephants and cheetahs,
the crocodiles and anteaters!"

Dad clapped his hands and said,
"Could we go by bus and buy **balloons?**
Eat ice creams and see **baboons?"**

"Yes, if you were very, **very** good," said Daisy,
"and behaved **exactly** as you should."

"And after the zoo, could we play in the park,
and stay out till it's really dark?"

Daisy folded her arms.

"We could go to the park but not for long . . .
You're so heavy and I'm not that strong."

"After the park I'd give you tea,
    with your friends and Mummy and Baby and me.

And you could play games like musical chairs,
and pass the parcel and hunt the bears."

"And then a bath to make me clean,
with ducks and bubbles and submarines?"

"I'd make you wash your face and hair,
behind your ears . . . everywhere!"

"And then I'd tuck you up in bed,
and give you a big kiss on your head."

Dad sighed, "What a day! I'd think I was dreaming –
no washing, no cooking, no driving, no cleaning!
Wouldn't it be great?"

Daisy looked at her dad.

She said, "Dad, if I were you and you were me . . .

...I think I'd rather be me!"